THIS IS THE FARM

ILLUSTRATIONS AND TEXT BY

Perrin Hendrick

(everything else by W. J. Trienens)

For Lizzy and Lucie with love and gratitude,

we *really* were working on a book...

This is the pig who looks to the sky,
wondering if it's a good day to fly.

This is the mouse who lives under the stairs,
borrowing your things for important affairs.

This is the goat who built his own boat,
with a ratio of sink greater than float.

This is the cat who ignores your affection,
she's planning the heist of a priceless collection.

This is the cow who wants you to know,
she just can't get into this season's new show.

This is the dog who begs your forgiveness,
he just couldn't stop—the villain who did this!

This is the turkey whose new umbrella just came,
patiently strutting while waiting for rain.

This is the sheep who was beamed into space,
to negotiate peace for the whole human race.

This is the donkey who's just a little hoarse,
on the night of his big performance—of course.

This is the rooster who stands on one leg,
contemplating the eternal chicken and egg.

This is the duck with the genius IQ,
whose new quantum theory is under review.

This is the squirrel who knows it sounds strange,
meet him here in a year—NO TIME TO EXPLAIN!

This is the horse who arouses suspicion,
he's a master of disguise on a top secret mission.

This is the rat who lives in the barn,
drawing conclusions with pictures and yarn.

This is the farm, more real than pretend,
this is the story and...

Visit us on the Web! laserpigpress.com

ISBN 978-0-692-17461-6

Text and Illustration by Perrin Hendrick

Book design by W. J. Trienens

The text for this book is set in Baskerville and White Wood

The illustrations for this book were rendered in watercolor and pen & ink.

CPSIA information can be obtained
at www.ICGtesting.com
Printed in the USA
LVIC061509130319
610513LV00007B/52